WARWICKSHIRE
Ghost Stories

Prepare to be frightened by these terrifying tales from around Warwickshire

By

Richard Holland

BRADWELL
BOOKS

Published by Bradwell Books
9 Orgreave Close Sheffield S13 9NP

Email: books@bradwellbooks.co.uk
All rights reserved. No part of this publication may be
reproduced, stored in a retrieval system or transmitted in any
form or by any means, electronic, mechanical, photocopying,
recording or otherwise without the prior permission
of Bradwell Books.
British Library Cataloguing in Publication Data: a catalogue
record for this book is available from the
British Library. 1st Edition

1st Edition

ISBN: 9781909914957

Print: Gomer Press, Llandysul, Ceredigion SA44 4JL

Design & Typesetting: jenksdesign@yahoo.co.uk

Photograph Credits: English Heritage, iStock and R. Holland
Front cover image of Baddesley Clinton: ©National Trust
Images/Andrew Butler

CONTENTS

Introduction	4
Haunted Houses	6
Creepy Castles	22
Holy Ghosts	32
Ghosts Around Town	46
Rural Hauntings	66

A view of Warwick Castle, surely the county's most impressive haunted location. iStock

INTRODUCTION

Warwickshire is in the heart of England, a beautiful and historic county, well blessed with handsome old towns and pretty villages. It boasts two of the UK's most impressive castles and a wealth of medieval houses and pubs, indicators of Warwickshire's early prosperity.

It is a county of gentle, undulating countryside, with lush meadows watered by the rivers Avon, Stour, Bourne and Itchen. The Cotswolds Area of Outstanding Natural Beauty extends into the southern part of the county. For centuries Warwickshire was largely covered in woodland, including the extensive Forest of Arden, whose name still crops up in many place names. Most of these trees were cut down to fuel the Industrial Revolution.

The Elizabethan playwright William Shakespeare is, of course, Warwickshire's most famous son, and he makes several references to the Forest of Arden in his works. Stratford-upon-Avon, Shakespeare's birthplace and long-time home, has capitalised on this connection since the 18th century. It has been the home of the Royal Shakespeare Company since 1961, although his plays had regularly been performed in the town's theatre since the late 19th century. Warwickshire is still sometimes known as 'Shakespeare Land'. There are numerous other connections, including at Charlecote Park, one of Warwickshire's many grand houses, where the young Shakespeare was reputedly caught poaching deer.

Nor is William Shakespeare Warwickshire's only literary connection. The Victorian writer George Eliot was born in

WARWICKSHIRE
Ghost Stories

Nuneaton and used the town as a model for provincial life in several of her novels, while First World War poet Rupert Brooke was born in Rugby.

Perhaps there is something in the Warwickshire air, for its residents seem to have always loved telling stories. The favourite fireside tales of the county's rural folk appear to have been ghost stories. If all these tales, and the first-hand accounts of modern witnesses, are to be believed, Warwickshire is a fearfully haunted county.

In such a historic county, this should perhaps come as no surprise. In Warwickshire was fought the first battle of the English Civil War, at Edge Hill, and the resonances of that fateful day still echo down the years. The old battleground is said to be haunted by spectral cavaliers. Other historical haunters include Lady Jane Grey and her father; Prince Rupert of the Rhine; St Editha, daughter of the Saxon King Egbert; and Piers Gaveston, favourite of King Edward II. Many more of its ghosts are of the local lords and ladies of past centuries. In addition, there are the more humble spooks: monks and nuns, maidservants, soldiers, clergymen, and even dogs.

The stories behind these hauntings can be fascinating, featuring as they do tragedies such as doomed romances and untimely deaths. Some of the personalities involved have such strength of character, it's no wonder memories of them have survived beyond the grave. Many lived lives of high drama or excess; some were killers, others victims. A few seem content to quietly haunt the places where they were once happiest.

I hope you enjoy this tour of one of England's most beautiful and most haunted counties.

HAUNTED HOUSES

A few miles south of Stratford-upon-Avon can be found the extensive grounds of Alscot Park. The house at its heart is an appealing blend of rococo and Gothic Revival architecture. It is still a private home but the estate has been developed to provide further homes, accommodation for businesses and space for a range of events.

An unknown female phantom has been seen in Alscot House, and two equally enigmatic figures, a man and a wife, are said to stroll up the drive and then melt away into thin air. Loud and inexplicable noises have also been heard in the drawing room, as if someone is knocking over the furniture and smashing the ornaments. As soon as the door is opened, the noises cease and everything is found to be in order.

The park has long had an eerie reputation. J. Harvey Bloom, the author of *Folklore, Old Customs and Superstitions in Shakespeare Land*, published in 1930, commented: 'One has the unpleasant sense of being dogged by something one cannot see and hardly hear.'

Those who have glimpsed this sinister presence have described it as a monster, a grotesque combination of man and calf. Possibly, however, the spook has some relation with the more orthodox apparition of a man which appears on the road past the entrance to the park. The figure manifests at midnight and always abruptly, as if someone had just switched on a light. These sudden appearances (and equally abrupt disappearances) have alarmed a number of motorists, who have swerved to avoid him. The ghost is thought to be of a farmer who, in order to win a bet, galloped his horse down the road at an unwise pace and collided with a low branch he had failed to notice in the dark. He was killed instantly. Presumably his ghost considers it safer to walk!

Alscot House, with its distinctive early Gothic Revival architecture, engraved in the mid-19th century. Both the house and its surrounding park are said to be haunted.

Baddesley Clinton, just north of Warwick, is one of the county's most fascinating properties. Now in the charge of the National Trust, Baddesley Clinton is a moated manor house dating back to the 13th century. It has long had a reputation for paranormal activity. During the 1800s, the then lady of the manor not only made a point of writing down any strange events in her diary but also invited the witnesses to sign and endorse the notes as true.

In 1884 a visitor staying in the Tapestry Room in Baddesley Clinton suddenly woke with an eerie feeling that she was not alone. She was astonished to see in her room a total stranger, a fair-haired woman dressed in black. She was more astonished still when the woman glided past her bed and vanished through the closed door. Three years later, on a return visit, she saw the ghost again. But on this occasion she was sleeping in the State Room. Suddenly waking during the night, she saw the same woman, illuminated in the bright moonlight that was shining through a window. The apparition was standing by a writing-desk, her face towards the witness, who described it as thoughtful and bearing similar features to those of her hosts, the Ferrers. The Ferrers family had owned Baddesley Clinton since the 16th century.

On subsequent occasions, a number of other witnesses, including guests and employees, have encountered this rather charming ghost, always in rooms or corridors on the upper storey. One visitor who returned to his room to fetch a book found her sitting there, bold as life. The lady's costume suggests that she dates from the 18th century, but which member of the Ferrers family she is remains open to conjecture.

A more certain identification is that of another defunct family member, Major Thomas Ferrers. Major Ferrers died abroad but his spirit seemed to find peace within the walls of the home he loved. His presence may be responsible for the mysterious footsteps which have been heard along an upstairs corridor.

It's uncertain whether Major Ferrers' ghost is also responsible for the heavy footsteps which disturbed the sleep of a Miss Henrietta Knight, who stayed at Baddesley Clinton in the early 1900s. Miss Knight was startled out of her sleep by the thumping of feet outside her door, as if half a dozen people were stumbling about in the corridor. This was followed by loud rappings on the walls and from the floor, and weird ripping sounds emanating from the empty air. Creepiest of all, Miss Knight also heard heavy breathing close to her bed. This unnerving experience presaged a period of poltergeist activity throughout the house. The noisy disturbances were eventually tamed by a service of exorcism.

The moated medieval manor house of Baddesley Clinton is haunted by two members of the family who owned the house for hundreds of years. iStock

The oddly named Barrells Hall, on the outskirts of the village of Ullenhall, is a Georgian-style house which has largely replaced an earlier mansion badly damaged in a fire in the 1930s. It is named after the Barrel family, who owned a house here in the Middle Ages. This was replaced by an Elizabethan mansion, built by a family named Knight. Barrells Hall's most famous – or I should say infamous – resident was Robert Knight, whose poor management of the South Sea Company caused the devastating 'South Sea Bubble' which ruined hundreds of investors. Knight was not affected; indeed he made a fortune out of the scam and escaped to France with it before he could be brought to account.

The ghost of Barrells Hall is thought to be another notable member of the 18th-century aristocracy, Henrietta Knight, Lady Luxborough. Henrietta became estranged from her husband and was effectively exiled to Barrells Hall, banned from approaching within twenty miles of either London or Bath, the two centres of fashionable society at the time. Undaunted, she created an exciting social milieu at her new home, surrounding herself with writers who became known as the 'Warwickshire Coterie'. Lady Luxborough was also a keen gardener and is credited with inventing the word 'shrubbery'.

During the years when Barrells Hall was an abandoned ruin, a ghostly woman wearing the fashions of the 18th century was occasionally glimpsed wandering round the area of the former gardens. On at least one occasion, she was also seen standing on the marble staircase in the midst of the ruin (one of the few remnants of the old hall still in good enough condition to be incorporated into the new house). Many have presumed this to be the apparition of the fascinating Henrietta Knight. As far as is known, the ghost has not been encountered for some time.

Charlecote Park is a magnificent Tudor manor house situated between Stratford-upon-Avon and Wellesbourne. Charlecote remained in the same hands – the Lucy family – from the 1200s, when an earlier house stood on the site, right up until 1945, when it was presented to the National Trust. The great ghost-hunter Peter Underwood spoke to a former owner, Lady

Barrells Hall, photographed before it suffered a devastating fire. Before its restoration, the ruined house was said to be haunted by a woman, possibly the shade of the highly cultured Lady Luxborough.

Fairfax-Lucy, who told him about 'an unidentifiable hubbub' which she and several members of her family heard coming from a small room in the west wing. Although no words could be made out, it sounded like a violent argument between a number of people, accompanied by thumps and crashes as if furniture was being knocked about. On investigation, the room was found to be empty, and it became silent as soon as the door was thrown open.

The apparition of a forlorn young woman has been seen making its way down to the lake in the grounds of Charlecote Park. This is believed to be the shade of a servant girl who drowned herself to escape some disgrace, perhaps the usual one of having become pregnant by some feckless man who then abandoned her. An entire book could be compiled of ghosts brought about by similar tragedies. This ghost girl is seen to throw herself into the lake and she then slips beneath the surface of the water, silently, having made no splash.

Although much of what is seen today dates from the 17th and the 19th centuries, a 15th-century mansion is at the core of Clopton House, a mile north of Stratford-upon-Avon. The house, which has now been converted into a series of private flats, was the family seat of the Cloptons, one of the wealthiest and most influential families in Warwickshire. Three tragedies in the life of the house have each resulted in a ghost. Margaret Clopton haunts the well at the rear of the property, into which she threw herself and drowned after a failed love affair 300 years ago. A bloody murder was committed in an attic room and this too is haunted, although it's unsure whether the gloomy presence is the victim or the remorseful killer.

The most horrifying incident, however, occurred in 1665. Plague came to Clopton and Charlotte, the pretty daughter of the house, beloved by all, was its first victim. She developed a high fever and in just a few days the physician had to break the sorrowful news that she was dead. The family and servants were all distraught, but such was their dread of the plague that Charlotte's interment in the crypt in nearby St Mary's Church was necessarily a hurried one without the pomp and ceremony which ordinarily would have been accorded her.

Sometime later another victim was claimed: Charlotte's mother. When the grieving family bore her body to the crypt, they were horrified to discover Charlotte, still wearing her shroud, huddled up against the door. The lid of her coffin was lying on the floor. Clearly, Charlotte had not been dead when they had buried her. She had succeeded in clawing her way out of her coffin but had been unable to escape the crypt or, presumably, to make herself heard. She had died a miserable, lonely death. When they found her corpse, the teeth were sunk into the arm, showing Charlotte had been in the last extremity of hunger when she'd died. Not surprisingly, her ghost too is said to walk the house.

WARWICKSHIRE
Ghost Stories

A 19th-century engraving of haunted Charlecote, an Elizabethan manor house now open to the public.

The National Trust also has the care of another splendid example of the Tudor manor house in Warwickshire, Coughton Court. Coughton Court is situated between Studley and Alcester, its impressive 16th-century gatehouse flanked by wings in the Gothic Revival style of the early 19th century. Like Charlecote, Coughton has been in the hands of the same family for centuries. The Throckmortons began living here in 1409 and still run the estate on behalf of the National Trust. Much plotting and scheming has gone on between Coughton's venerable walls: in 1538 the Throckmortons plotted to remove Queen Elizabeth I from the throne and, in 1605, two of the Gunpowder Plot conspirators – each married to a Throckmorton daughter – hid here after their failed attempt to blow up the Houses of Parliament.

The disembodied footsteps heard hurrying through the house are thought to belong to the latter incident, although there is, of course, no way to substantiate it. They always follow the same course: down the main staircase, through the drawing room and towards the south-west turret. Here they cease, perhaps revealing the place where one or more of the conspirators attempted to conceal themselves from justice.

Considered so spooky that it became the uncredited star of, in my opinion, the best supernatural thriller ever filmed, Ettington Park's high Gothic architecture still has the ability to impress. Ettington Park stood in for Hill House in Robert Wise's 1963 movie *The Haunting*, a superbly atmospheric and unnervingly convincing adaptation of Shirley Jackson's ghost story, *The Haunting of Hill House*. The house – now Ettington Park Hotel – was given an extensive makeover in the 1850s, transforming it into the strikingly ornate, fake medieval concoction we can enjoy today. Now it too has a haunted reputation rivalling that of the fictional Hill House.

During the filming of *The Haunting*, actor Russ Tamblyn claimed to have had an eerie experience one night in the grounds of Ettington Park. Unable to sleep, he was wandering round behind the house when he was struck by a feeling as if a block of ice had descended on his head, the cold trickling down through his body. He was convinced that something rather than someone was looking at him, and he hurried back inside without waiting to find out what it might be.

By the time of Mr Tamblyn's experience, the house was already rumoured to be haunted by a woman in a white gown. This ghost is now known as 'Lady Emma'. She has been seen in various parts of the house, including the main hall, where she vanished through a solid wall, indicating that she may pre-date the Victorian remodelling of the house. Later reports speak of 'a girl dressed in the costume of the 12th century' also being seen in the house. Further apparitions have been claimed for Ettington Park since it became a hotel. These include a servant girl who was pushed down the main staircase and broke her neck; an older woman in a black Victorian gown; two children who drowned in the stretch of the River Stour which runs through the estate; and a monk who wanders the grounds, perhaps in the mistaken belief that the house is really the medieval abbey it's pretending to be.

Few places in England are so steeped in legend as Guy's Cliffe, a hamlet between Warwick and Leek Wootton. It is named after Guy of Warwick, a hero who appeared in a number of medieval romances and later novels. The legends state that Guy was of low birth, but fell in love with the 'Lady Felice' (whose name means 'happiness'). In order to win this aristocratic woman's hand, he needed to prove himself worthy of her by becoming a knight. This he achieved by fighting valiantly in many battles and by slaying giants, dragons and other fearsome, fantastical creatures.

The striking gatehouse admitting entrance into Coughton Court, a house of intrigue with a ghost linked to the Gunpowder Plot. iStock

At length the longed-for marriage between Guy and the Lady Felice came to pass. Yet, despite being wedded to 'happiness', Guy was still unhappy. Feeling remorse over his violent past, he decided to purge his sins by going on pilgrimage to the Holy Land. Even this was not enough to make Guy feel good about himself, however, and, without telling Lady Felice he'd arrived back home, he became a hermit and lived in a cave perched on a cliff above the River Avon. Eventually his wife tracked him down but only in time to nurse him through his final illness. He died in the arms of the woman he had fought so hard to win but whom he never felt worthy of his love. The place where the pious hero had his hermitage is now known as Guy's Cliffe. The area is said to be haunted by the distraught spirit of Guy's heartbroken widow, the Lady Felice.

At the heart of the former Guy's Cliffe estate was a big country house, built in the 18th century. For many years Guy's Cliffe House stood empty and neglected, falling into disrepair (Warwickshire seems to have an inordinate number of such properties within its borders). It soon took on the appearance of the archetypal haunted house. Although it stood on private property, for a time people interested in history or those who could take pleasure in a melancholy ruin would visit the shell of Guy's Cliffe House and a few came away telling of being overcome by an unearthly cold and the sense that 'something terrible' was near them. One visitor who experienced the oppressive atmosphere of the place said she also saw 'a giant black figure towering over her'. The figure was no more than a silhouette, but she ran away from it so quickly that it's unlikely she would have been able to make out any identifying features anyway.

Lawford Hall fared even less well than Guy's Cliffe House, for now nothing remains of it. Originally situated at Little

Lawford, the house was demolished many years ago. It used to be haunted by a busy ghost named 'One-Handed Boughton'. The Boughtons were the owners of Lawford Hall for centuries. It's uncertain why this particular Boughton lost his hand: some say it was amputated after an accident during the reign of Good Queen Bess, others that he dates back to Saxon times and that his hand was amputated as a punishment for unlawfully extending the boundaries between his and his neighbours' lands. One-Handed Boughton had the habit of racing round the perimeter of Lawford Hall's estate in a spectral coach. Often he drove the horses himself, wildly whipping them into a frenzy, his scarlet cloak billowing behind him.

His troublesome ghost also haunted Lawford Hall itself, terrorising the servants and keeping everyone up at night with its antics. Eventually a dozen clergymen, including four bishops, got together to perform an exorcism on One-Handed Boughton and, after a great struggle, succeeded in conjuring his spirit into a bottle. This was only achieved after making the concession that the ghost could continue to wander the house and his estate for two hours a night. Then the bottle was thrown into a pool near the house. One-Handed Boughton made the most of his freedom to continue to alarm the household and the neighbouring countryside.

In 1790 Lawford Hall was sold to the Caldecote family, who immediately pulled it down 'as a thing accursed'. Twenty years later, the bottle allegedly containing One-Handed Boughton's spirit happened to be fished out of the pond. Its discovery created great interest in the county and it was put on public exhibition in Rugby. Then it was returned to the Boughton family, who by this time were living at Brownsover Hall, just outside Rugby. To their dismay, One-Handed Boughton now began to haunt their new home instead! As late as the 1940s, the bottle was still in the hands of the family, but when they quitted the house in the 1940s they sealed it up in a secret location within the walls. One-Handed Boughton then grew much quieter and hasn't been heard of for some time. Brownsover Hall is now a hotel.

An old photo of Guy's Cliffe House. The surrounding area is said to be haunted by the grieving Lady Felice. After the house fell into disrepair, it too gained a haunted reputation.

Fortunately still with us is Ragley Hall, one of Warwickshire's grandest stately homes. The house was built in 1680 and is an early example of Palladian architecture, a style which became more established during the reigns of the Georges. It's a particularly handsome example and was designed by Robert Hooke, who made his name as a chemist and pioneering microscopist before turning with considerable success to architecture. The grounds were laid out by the equally noted landscape gardener Capability Brown. Ragley Hall has been owned by the Seymour family, the Earls of Hertford, since it was built. The house and gardens are open to the public.

Although the house is not in itself haunted, the grounds can boast not one but three 'White Ladies'. According to *Folklore, Old Customs and Superstitions of Shakespeare Land* by J. Harvey Bloom, a thrilling, if somewhat grisly, discovery was made in Ragley Park in 1833: the skeleton of a woman dating from the Anglo-Saxon period. The first White Lady is presumably the ghost of this woman, for she materialises over the grave.

Tradition states that the second White Lady was in life a maidservant employed at Ragley Hall in the late 18th century. She was beloved by the Italian valet of the then Marquis of Hertford. It's uncertain whether she returned his affection, for he was frightfully jealous of anyone else paying her any attention and seemed indeed to be morbidly obsessed with the girl. One day, the pair of them vanished from the hall. At first it was assumed they had eloped together, but shortly after their disappearance the apparition of the missing maidservant began to be seen wandering the grounds. Now it was feared that the valet had killed her in a jealous rage and possibly buried her body somewhere in the grounds. At any rate, neither of them was seen again – except the girl, of course, in ghostly form. Like the others, she wears a long, white gown like a wedding dress.

The third White Lady cannot be mistaken for the others, for she is seen riding an equally phantom horse, white to match her dress. She gallops through the moonlight, leaping a spring (near where the Anglo-Saxon skeleton was found) before she and the horse both wink out of existence beside an old oak tree.

On the other side of this tree there runs a lane which is also haunted. However, the ghost that patrols it is not seen, merely heard. It appears to be some form of large animal, padding invisibly through the dark.

Just off the A425 east of Southam is Shuckburgh Hall, an old country house with an Italianate frontage added in the 1840s. Tragedy struck Shuckburgh when Lucy, the daughter of a former owner, Sir William Stewkley, was murdered by her lover, a Lieutenant Sharp. Sharp appears to have been left unhinged after a tour of duty during the Napoleonic Wars, and may have carried out this extreme act because he had been banned from seeing Lucy. After he had shot the unfortunate girl, he turned his gun on himself and blew his own brains out. The young couple are said to haunt the environs of Shuckburgh Hall, strolling arm in arm. As well as the house, their main haunt is the path up to Napton-on-the-Hill, where the tragedy happened.

Studley Castle, near Redditch, is now a hotel. Despite its castellated appearance, it is actually a Victorian house in the Gothic style, complete with fake towers. Julia Skinner, in her *Haunted Warwickshire: Ghost Stories*, tells another tragic tale about this grand house. From one of these towers, she writes, a crazed former owner threw his child to its death, convinced that his wife had been unfaithful to him and that he was not its father. His wronged and grief-stricken wife ran out of the house and drowned herself in the lake. She has haunted Studley Castle ever since.

The grounds of Ragley Hall are haunted by three ladies in white and something eerily invisible. iStock

CREEPY CASTLES

Warwick Castle is one of the most magnificent and beautifully situated medieval fortresses in England. Indeed, Walter Scott, that great populariser of all things medieval, described it as 'the fairest monument of ancient chivalrous splendor which yet remains uninjured by time'.

Warwick Castle stands on a sandstone bluff overlooking a crook in the River Avon, the waters reflecting its mighty walls and towers. The site was developed shortly after the Norman Conquest but the splendid edifice we see today dates mainly from the 14th century. The castle was converted into a country house in the 17th century by the Greville family, members of whom held the title of Earl of Warwick.

Today Warwick Castle is a major tourist attraction. In addition to the historic interest of the castle and the fine interiors of the mansion it became, the crowds also flock here to see the many medieval re-enactments, shows and other events regularly staged in the grounds. After dark, Warwick Castle takes on a new aspect, a decidedly spooky one. A considerable amount of paranormal activity has been reported from within its walls.

The man who set about converting the stern fortress into a comfortable country house, Sir Fulke Greville, is one of Warwick's traditional ghosts. Greville was murdered by his valet, who stabbed his master in a rage while helping him to dress. Greville had just made his will and left a modest bequest to his valet, who clearly considered it way too modest. The murder happened in London, but Greville's spirit is said to have returned to the place where he had spent so much time

Stunning Warwick Castle is haunted by the aristocratic Sir Fulke Greville, the man who converted it into a stately home. iStock

and money making it a home. He now haunts the Watergate Tower (also known as the 'Ghost Tower'), in the suite of rooms which formerly included his study.

Considered to be unrelated to the presence of Sir Fulke Greville are the disembodied footsteps which pace the so-called Japanese Corridor. They have been heard for many years and by numerous – occasionally multiple – witnesses. A former Countess of Warwick, whose Writing Room opened onto the Japanese Corridor, often heard the footsteps. She got quite used to returning to the locked room, only to find that the papers on her desk had been shifted about as if someone had been reading through her notes. One night during the First World War, an American guest heard the footsteps approaching him down the otherwise empty corridor. Fascinated, he held his ground as the steps 'walked' right up to him – and then through him. This eerie experience was too much for his nerves, however, and he hurried off to his room, locking the door behind him.

The third ghost story of Warwick Castle concerns a troublesome woman named Moll Bloxham. Moll had been a maid at the castle but in her declining years was settled in a cottage nestling below its walls and given the means to earn a modest living by selling any milk and butter not used each day by the kitchens. Despite receiving these comestibles free of charge, Moll cheated her customers by selling short measures and using dodgy scales, weighted to her advantage. Eventually, news of this reached the Earl of Warwick's ears and he immediately withdrew the concession from his ungrateful servant. What happened next is uncertain: she presumably died, either of starvation or of pique. Afterwards, the story insists, she began to haunt Warwick Castle in the form of a fearsome black dog.

The huge spectral hound would wander the castle after dark, filling with dread anyone who encountered it. Three clergymen were called in to try to exorcise the spook. With bell, book and candle, they pursued Moll's bestial spirit through the castle until, at last, it was trapped on top of the tallest of its towers. Unable to withstand the holiness being directed at it, the hound jumped from the tower and into the River Avon below. It was swept away by the current and became trapped beneath the dam, where, according to the legend, it remains, still furious and anxious to escape.

An old engraving of Warwick Castle. A phantom dog leapt from the castle's tallest tower after being pursued by exorcists. iStock

Despite being little more than an empty shell, Kenilworth Castle is almost as impressive as Warwick, indeed its ruinous condition only seems to add to its romance. It size and magnificence reflect its importance in English history. The first castle was built in the 1120s. It was greatly enlarged by King John and enlarged again by one of its most famous former owners, John of Gaunt. John of Gaunt made Kenilworth as much a palace as a fortress and this impression was further enhanced in the 16th century by the Earl of Leicester, who raised Tudor-style apartments here.

Unfortunately, during the Civil War, Parliamentarian forces set about wrecking Kenilworth Castle so that it couldn't be used again by the Royalist opposition, and this explains its shattered state today. Somewhat cheekily, one of Cromwell's officers, a Colonel Hawksworth, had the castle's gatehouse repaired in 1650 and turned it into a home for himself. For this reason it is one of the few parts of the complex that still has a roof over it. In her book *Haunted Warwickshire*, author Meg Elizabeth Atkins describes a weird incident in this building.

One pleasant summer's evening, a folk band were performing in the Gatehouse. To her amazement, a member of the audience saw the figure of a woman materialise beside them. She was young, fine-featured and wearing a simple headdress and a gown of some pale material. The apparition was placidly sitting and sewing in the light shining through a big, mullioned window behind the band. The vision lasted a few seconds before fading. One of the witness's friends knew a woman who had an interest in historical costume. On hearing a description of the ghost's clothing, the expert pronounced that the style was similar to that of the 14th century. The identity of the phantom lady remains unknown, however.

The castle is also haunted by a spectral coach. Pulled by four equally spectral horses, the coach erupts out of the southern gate and rattles away over the lake where a causeway used to be. It vanishes in the direction of Warwick. Kenilworth Castle is now administered by English Heritage and is open to the public.

The haunted gatehouse of Kenilworth Castle rises behind a cottage on the outskirts of the town. iStock

In the village of Baginton, near Coventry, can be found the scanty remains of a medieval fortress, Bagot's Castle, named after the important family who owned it. In the late 1300s the Bagots enlarged and improved a castle originally built two centuries before and made it their base of operations. The castle ruins are managed by a local community trust and there are plans to excavate the site further.

Bagot's Castle was abandoned as early as the 16th century and quickly became derelict. By the 1930s the fortress had long since vanished from view, presenting no more to the eye than vague lumps in a grassy field. In 1934, a team of amateur archaeologists got together to excavate the remains. As they began their work, they got wind of a certain antipathy from some of the locals. The reason for this surprised them: the residents were afraid that their digging would disturb an angry ghost.

The ghost story, as related by Rupert Matthews in his *Haunted Places of Warwickshire*, is an interesting one. The yarn tells of a lovely young heiress abducted by a cruel member of the Bagot family, who imprisoned her in the castle and tried to bully her into marrying him, so that he could claim her vast estates. She refused, holding out against him until eventually his brutality and her isolation proved too much for her and she died, alone and miserable in the depths of the castle. After her death, her spirit sought revenge on the inhabitants of Bagot Castle and also the neighbouring villagers, apparently because no one had come to her aid during her ordeal. According to Mr Matthews, her ghost did indeed walk again once the excavations of her former prison were under way.

Considered quite separate from this ghost is the phantom of a woman in a cloak which has also been seen in the village. It glides along a path leading to the churchyard and then out the other side, before vanishing near the Old Rectory. Who it is, nobody knows.

A female figure also haunts the ruins of Hartshill Castle. The original castle was used by Henry Tudor as his HQ before the Battle of Bosworth, which secured for him the Crown of England. The walls still standing today belong to an

The mighty ruins of Kenilworth Castle are haunted by two very different ghosts.
iStock

Elizabethan mansion which replaced it. The ghost, judging by her costume, dates from the same period as the mansion. Dressed head to foot in black, she was considered 'best avoided' by the locals. When Hartshill Castle was being excavated some years ago, a mouldering skeleton was found in the foundations, squeezed into a coffin-sized brick-lined hole. This peculiar last resting place suggested that perhaps this was a victim of murder and may well therefore explain the presence of the ghostly woman in black.

For many years Astley Castle was also a ruin, standing forlorn and neglected among the trees, cut off from the world by its moat. A medieval fortified manor house, it was badly damaged by fire in the 1970s and then abandoned. Recently, it has been given new life as a holiday home by the Landmark Trust, who have carefully constructed stylish accommodation within its remaining walls. This is a historic place, the former home of the ill-fated Lady Jane Grey, the 'Nine Days Queen'. A committed Protestant, Lady Jane was pressured into becoming queen on the death of Edward VI in 1553 in a bid to keep a Roman Catholic off the throne. She only survived in her elevated role from 10 July to 19 July, before being removed by the legitimate heir, Mary I. Lady Jane Grey was executed for high treason on 12 February 1554, aged just 17.

Lady Jane is one of the ghosts said to haunt Astley Castle. The other is her father, Henry Grey, the Duke of Suffolk. For his part in placing his daughter on the throne, and, more seriously, for being part of a plot to assassinate Queen Mary before she had a chance to marry Philip of Spain (a match which ultimately failed to occur), Henry became a fugitive. For several days he hid in a hollow oak tree on the Astley Castle estate, before being given away by a keeper, who claimed his cash reward as Henry was dragged away to be beheaded. Henry's ghost is apparently headless, but Jane – who famously kept her head throughout her ordeal – has retained hers.

Maxstoke Castle, in the portion of the county that skirts Birmingham, is a 14th-century castle long since converted to a comfortable private home, but one which has maintained its original appearance to a remarkable degree. It houses a number of historical relics of great interest, in particular the table round which the Gunpowder Plot was planned and an ancient chair on which Henry Tudor was crowned after the Battle of Bosworth in 1485. Maxstoke Castle is usually open to the public once a year to raise money for charities.

According to Meg Elizabeth Atkins, Maxstoke Castle has a haunted staircase, 'the scene of a duel in which a member of the family slew his brother in a quarrel about a bag of gold'.

WARWICKSHIRE
Ghost Stories

Lady Jane Grey, whose ghost haunts her former home, Astley Castle, along with that of her father. iStock

Mrs Atkins adds that the castle is also possessed of a door which has the unaccountable habit of 'flying open at midnight'.

HOLY GHOSTS

Warwickshire is remarkably rich in haunted churches. A number of these are associated with castles and great houses which are also believed to be haunted.

At one time a wealthy priory adjoined Kenilworth Castle. It was founded in 1122 by the same man who built the original castle, Geoffrey de Clinton. Despite its former magnificence, little remains above ground now of Kenilworth Priory, but its foundations and a few walls are visible in Abbey Fields (the priory was given abbey status in the final century of its existence). On the other side of Abbey Fields from the castle is Kenilworth's parish church. A procession of phantom monks has been seen making its way from St Nicholas's Church and then down through the avenue of trees leading to Abbey Fields. At the end of the avenue, they turn left and vanish at the spot where the entrance to Kenilworth Priory formerly stood. Townsfolk have also reported hearing monkish chanting emanating from the Abbey Fields.

Close to Astley Castle is St Mary's Church, whose graveyard is also haunted by a monk-like figure. The shadowy form has been observed gliding between the headstones, its face obscured by a hood.

St Michael's Church, Baddesley Clinton, was built at about the same time as the nearby moated manor house. It stands in a shady glade a short walk up from the house. The interior contains two interesting memorials to Sir Edward Ferrers of Baddesley Clinton, who died in 1535: a brightly painted table tomb and a stained glass window depicting Sir Edward with his widow, Lady Constance.

Before the Ferrers moved into Baddesley Clinton, it belonged to the Brome family. One of these, Nicholas Brome, was a real firebrand. He kept up a running feud with his neighbour, the Squire of Longbridge, in the closing years of the War of the Roses. Brome had supported the House of York, his neighbour the Lancastrians. On one occasion, Brome rode to Longbridge, hacked down anyone who stood in his way and killed the squire, before riding away again. This solo raid caused the newly crowned Henry IV (who belonged neither to the House of York nor that of Lancaster) to clamp down on the feud and to have Brome arrested and fined.

Alas, this did not change Brome's ways. A particularly grim episode occurred when he returned home unexpectedly to Baddesley Clinton to see the family priest chucking his wife under the chin. His quick temper inflamed, he drew his sword and killed the overly familiar cleric on the spot. In penance for this crime, Brome had the tower built on to St Michael's Church. On his death, in an act of eternal humility, his body was buried under a stone just outside the church door so that people would tread on him as they went in to their devotions.

Nicholas Brome now haunts the churchyard. His tall figure, dressed in medieval garb, strides up through the woods and down the path to the church door. He vanishes on the stone covering his grave. Some say he only visits St Michael's Church once every ten years (his next appearance being due in 2017), but there is evidence his ghost has been seen more often than that.

Spectral monks have been seen at St Nicholas's Church, Kenilworth. iStock

It is a very different sort of personality who haunts Little Compton Church. The parish church is a distinctive building, boasting an unusual 'hip-roofed' tower. It also has an unusual dedication, to St Denys, the patron saint of France. This is because the church originally belonged to the Abbey of St Denys, in Paris. In the 19th century, a shy young curate was employed at the church. Mr Drane was deeply in love with a beautiful girl in the choir who had the voice of an angel. Unfortunately, he was not the only admirer of the lovely Miss Fielding. Far from it. Among her many suitors was a Captain Brandon, who owned one of the local big houses, the Grange, and it was no surprise to anyone when she plumped for this wealthy bachelor.

Mr Drane's devotion to Miss Fielding had been no secret; indeed it had been something of a shared joke among the congregation. It was therefore thoughtless at best when she insisted that he conduct the ceremony at her wedding. The young curate performed his duties admirably. His voice barely shook, he stumbled over the words perhaps just once or twice. At the end of the service, he kissed the bride, wished her well for the future and cheerily waved the couple out of the churchyard. Then he returned quietly to the silent church, and hanged himself in the belfry. The spectre of the tragic little curate is said to linger on at St Denys, and has been spotted watching wedding parties with a mournful expression.

Another sad spirit haunts the churchyard and surrounding lanes at Brailes. In the shadow of St George's splendid, 120-feet-high tower, the ghost of a sorrowing young woman has been seen. When the girl became pregnant, and then abandoned by her lover, her parents tried to hush up the incident and kept her confined until the baby was born. Then they snatched the infant from her arms and had it sent off to relatives far away. This only added to their unfortunate daughter's distress. She went into a decline and died of a broken heart.

Distressingly similar is the apparition of a grieving young widow of the Civil War period which is seen in the lane leading to St Laurence's Church, Lighthorne. She had only been married a few months when her husband, fired by Puritan zeal, ran off to join Cromwell's army, which was then massing at Edge Hill to take on the forces of King Charles I. Sadly, he was one of the many killed in this bloody battle. A neighbour caught up with his wife and broke the bad news to her as she was making her way down Church Lane to pray at St Laurence's. The shock was too much for her. She collapsed, wailing uncontrollably, and for months after the tragedy would return to the spot where she had learnt of her husband's death, staring vacantly around her. It is in this aspect that she is most often seen, standing grim and white-faced, but her wails of grief have been heard, too.

Yet another female phantom has been encountered in the vicinity of the church at Harbury. She walks from All Saints Church, into the village, carrying a baby in her arms. The apparition vanishes at the spot where she and her child were killed in an accident many years ago.

The ghost of an elderly lady with a rolled-up umbrella makes her way up to, rather than away from, the windswept ancient church which serves Napton-on-the-Hill. There seems to be no tragedy attached to her; presumably she is simply retracing the steps she took many times before in life on her way to worship. Within the church two more enigmatic women have been seen. Dressed in the high fashion of the Tudor period, in ruffs and headdresses, they sit in the front pew, apparently in

St Michael's Church, Baddesley Clinton, is haunted by medieval bad boy Nicholas Brome. iStock

prayer. No one knows who they are but the ghosts have earned the reputation of being bad omens. It is said their appearance presages misfortune to anyone who sees them.

A family of ghosts is said to visit the graveyard of St John the Baptist's Church in Wolvey every July. In the 18th century a Gypsy girl shocked her tribe by leaving and settling down with a Wolvey man. Sadly, the marriage ended in tragedy. The girl died giving birth to her first child, and the baby was stillborn. The young widower was understandably distraught and he never recovered. Every day he would make a pilgrimage to the grave where his beloved and their baby were buried. On the precise anniversary of the tragedy, the man's lifeless body was found collapsed over the grave. A few days later, he was buried with his wife and child. Every July – the month in which their deaths occurred – the ghosts of the young couple and their baby return to Wolvey churchyard.

St Nicholas's, the parish church of Alcester (more of which in the next chapter) is something of an oddity. At first glance it appears to be a typical medieval church but most of what you see is little more than a century old, erected to replace the exterior of an 18th-century church, designed to look like a Greek temple, which had itself replaced the 13th-century edifice originally on the site.

St Nicholas's Church is said to be haunted by Sir Fulke Greville, whose ghost is the one most active in Warwick Castle. Sir Fulke belonged to Alcester parish, so was buried here after his untimely death at the hands of his crazed valet. He is so busy haunting Warwick Castle that he is seldom seen in Alcester, merely appearing briefly beside the tomb dedicated to him and his wife. In his *Haunted Places of Warwickshire*, Rupert Matthews describes Sir Fulke's ghost as being 'dressed in a dark suit of beautiful velvet and sporting a wide ruff of snow-white linen'.

The original church was also briefly haunted by an angry monk named Ansel. Ansel had been a monk at Alcester's Benedictine Abbey during the reign of Stephen and Matilda. For some reason now lost in the mists of time, King Stephen had Ansel arrested and then executed. With his dying breath, the monk cursed the abbey, saying: 'The tyrant's church shall fall.' His vengeful spirit afterwards haunted the abbey and for three centuries was blamed for a series of misfortunes, including the steady collapse of the buildings, epidemics and violent behaviour by the brothers.

King Henry VI got so fed up with the bad reports about Alcester Abbey that he decided to kick out all the monks. The abbey was reduced to the comparatively modest status of priory instead. However, it wasn't until the eventual Dissolution of the Monasteries under Henry VIII that Ansel felt himself appeased. His spirit appeared in St Nicholas's Church and directed a group of priests who happened to be gathered there to the resting place of his bones. He ordered them to dig them up and rebury them in consecrated ground. This they did and the curse was lifted. Nothing now remains above ground of Alcester Abbey.

There is no doubt about the authenticity of St Peter's Church, Wootton Wawen. It is believed to be the oldest church in Warwickshire. Its Saxon interior is remarkably well preserved, although this is now entirely surrounded by a later medieval fabric. Old though it is, St Peter's Church stands on an even older site, associated with the Romans, who set up a camp here. A prominent lump in the graveyard might perhaps be a burial mound of the Roman or prehistoric periods, or possibly

St Nicholas's Church, Alcester, is one of two places in Warwickshire haunted by the murdered Sir Fulke Greville. iStock

a mound raised to elevate a preaching cross which would have brought worshippers here prior to the building of the church.

The phantom of the churchyard is a dramatic one. In 1742, William Somerville was buried at Wootton Wawen. At the time he was the squire of nearby Edstone, but was known nationally as a poet. He was something of a wild character, an enthusiastic huntsman addicted to the chase (as expressed in one of his best-remembered poems, 'The Chase'). Legend has it that if a hunting horn is sounded within earshot of St Peter's churchyard, Squire Somerville's ghost will immediately leap out of his grave, mounted on a spectral steed, and thunder away in pursuit of the fox.

Not far from the church is the site of a Benedictine priory. The monastic house was founded shortly after the Norman Conquest and was peopled exclusively with monks from France. The priory was endowed with the village and estates of Wootton Wawen in order to provide them with an income. The French monks' inability to converse with their Saxon neighbours interfered not one jot with their ability to collect their rents, and their foreignness (which wasn't their fault) and their greed (which was) made them decidedly unpopular. Indeed, so unpopular did they become that the Bishop of Lichfield closed down the priory and packed each and every *frère* back home. The villagers swiftly took their revenge by demolishing the priory and reusing the building material for their own homes and farms until there was not a stone left above ground. However, the banished monks have not quite quit Wootton Wawen: their shades are still to be glimpsed, usually just after dawn, either singly in the field where the priory once stood or making their way in silent procession up to St Peter's Church.

The church at Wootton Wawen is not the only one in Warwickshire to be haunted by a sporting gentleman. Edward Golding was the parish clerk at Ilmington about 250 years ago and shared Squire Somerville's fondness for riding to hounds. By his own estimation, he neglected his duties in favour of his sporting pursuits and ordered to have carved on his tomb within St Mary's Church the epitaph, 'His performance of the duties of his office fell far short of their obligations and importance.' His ghost is characteristically dressed in a long riding coat, as if he can't wait to get back out to the chase.

One witness saw his apparition approaching her as she was arranging flowers on the altar. A friend of hers recounted her experience to ghost-hunter Andrew Green: 'As he got near her,' she said, 'he faded away as if one was turning off a television programme.'

Polesworth's parish church was originally part of an abbey founded in AD 827 by King Egbert. Its official name is the Abbey Church of St Editha, dedicated to Egbert's daughter, who served as its first abbess. In addition to the church a handsome gatehouse survives from the 14th century. As is well known, Henry VIII closed down England's monastic houses and, more often than not, gave or sold their lands to favoured noblemen. Local bigwig Francis Goodere acquired Polesworth Abbey after the Dissolution and decided to pull down most of its buildings in order to recycle the stone for use in his new house, Polesworth Hall (which was itself demolished in the 19th century). During the demolition of Polesworth Abbey, St Editha's ghost is said to have appeared, glowering at the workmen who were carrying out the desecration. Terrified out of their wits, the labourers downed tools for a while but were eventually coaxed back to complete the work with the winning combination of threats and cash.

Although she was unable to prevent the destruction of her beloved abbey, St Editha's spirit is believed to still return to its location from time to time. Wearing a sorrowful expression, the abbess has been seen walking slowly from the Abbey Church to the gatehouse.

The Church of St Mary the Virgin peeps from behind the honey-coloured cottages of Ilmington. The church is haunted by a former parish clerk. iStock

The grand medieval cathedral of Coventry (now formally part of the West Midlands unitary authority) was one of 60,000 buildings destroyed in a brutal bombing campaign carried out by the Luftwaffe during the Second World War. When the city centre was being rebuilt after the war, it was decided to build a new cathedral and to leave the shell of the original structure as a kind of anti-war memorial. For several years, it was reported that aircraft could be heard droning in the skies above the cathedral at 2am. A few people even claimed to see spotlights raking the clouds, although no such equipment had been in operation since VE Day. It appeared to the witnesses that they were experiencing again the moments before the devastating bombing, which took place at 2am on 14 November 1940. Today, paranormal researchers refer to such playbacks as 'time slips'.

However, these possible time slips are not the only spooky experiences reported from the cathedral. Another strange event was recounted in the *Coventry Herald*, dated 20 January 1893. David McGrory reprints an excerpt from the news story in his book *Haunted Coventry*:

'A few minutes to ten o'clock, the choir was practising funeral hymns … in memoriam of the late Alderman Dalton [a recently deceased churchwarden]. "Blessed are the Dead" was being sung, and the verger was at the west end of the church. Suddenly his attention was called to an object described as an arm holding aloft "a torch of bright blue flame". The object started from the north aisle. It proceeded down the aisle till Mr Dalton's former pew was reached. Then it disappeared, and [junior verger, Tom] Owen's searchings were in vain.

'But a few minutes later he asked a choirman if he had seen the light, and immediately the choirman testifies "it" again appeared at the spot where Owen saw it disappear the first time, and went along the church to the south-west corner, among the bells etc. that lie there. The verger went to the spot, but to no purpose.'

The assumption on the part of the witnesses was that the spirit of the late Alderman Dalton had been among them, summoned as it were by the run-through of his own memorial service.

For a few years after the Second World War, people walking past the bombed-out shell of Coventry Cathedral claimed to have experienced a 'time slip' taking them back to the terrible night when the Luftwaffe targeted the city. iStock

GHOSTS ABOUT TOWN

We have already visited Warwick's mighty castle, but there are several other haunted properties in this historic town. Right up against the castle wall can be found Oken House, a timber-framed Tudor mansion named after a former owner, Thomas Oken. Oken's was a rags to riches story; he rose from an impoverished background to become one of Warwick's richest merchants. For many years Thomas Oken was said to still be seen in his former home, most often on the main staircase. Sometimes only his footsteps were heard, clumping down the stairs. The attractive black-and-white building is now the Thomas Oken Tearooms.

Huddled against the medieval West Gate into the town is the venerable Lord Leycester Hospital, which dates back to the late 1300s. This fascinating building started life as a religious house belonging to guildsmen of the town. It was turned into a hospital under the patronage of Robert Dudley, Earl of Leicester (rumoured to have been the lover of Good Queen Bess) and today is a retirement home for ex-servicemen.

That rather unlikely staple of traditional folklore, the headless ghost, used to stalk Lord Leycester Hospital after dark. No one knew who it was, because there was no face available to identify it. But then one day a remarkable discovery was made. Workmen carrying out repairs found a cavity in a wall of the Chapel of St James at the top of the West Gate. Inside was the headless skeleton of a man in medieval armour. Who he was, why he was hidden in the chapel, or what dark deed or tragedy lies behind this extraordinary interment are questions that are unlikely ever to be answered. But one thing now seems certain – whoever he may have been in life, it was his ghost which had taken to wandering round the Lord Leycester. As soon as the body was given a decent burial, the ghost vanished, never to be seen again.

In an article in the *Daily Mail*, dated 17 June 2011, television presenter Anne Diamond related a spooky experience she had in 1999 while house-hunting in Warwick. An estate agent directed her to a Victorian family house near the castle, where she was shown round by its owner, a little old lady with snow-white hair. They chatted amiably during the tour and Mrs Diamond decided that the place was just right for her and her four sons. She was disappointed to be later told that the owner had changed her mind about selling because she couldn't bear to part with the place. So, the house-hunting continued.

Nothing else seemed quite suitable and Anne Diamond never forgot the house in Warwick: she'd fallen in love with it. She was excited when, about six months later, she was informed that the house had come back on the market. She lost no time in arranging another viewing and this time she took her mother with her. They were given keys to let themselves in so were a little surprised when the door opened and they were invited inside by the owner, the same elderly lady Mrs Diamond had met on their first visit.

'You know the layout,' she said, 'so I'll leave you to show yourselves around.' She then shuffled off in the direction of the kitchen. The light was fading, but when the house-hunters tried the lights they found the electricity had been disconnected. They called for the owner, but got no reply. It seemed odd that the woman should leave them alone to wander round in the dark, but they persevered. In the living room, Mrs Diamond's mother sat down on something in one of the murky rooms and chatted with her daughter about the suitability of the house. Then she noticed something odd about the box-like thing she was sitting on.

'I don't like this, it looks like a coffin,' she said.

Although not normally superstitious, mother and daughter were suddenly overcome with an eerie feeling and, in Anne Diamond's words, they both 'bolted for the front door'. One can imagine how they felt when the estate agent told them the next day that the owner couldn't possibly have let them in, since she had died a few weeks previously! The house was standing empty, cleared of its furniture by the deceased's children. Not surprisingly, Anne Diamond's house-hunting continued elsewhere.

A headless ghost used to patrol the medieval Lord Leycester Hospital in Warwick.
iStock

Although it is now part of the West Midlands, Coventry formerly belonged to Warwickshire and is just a few miles north of Warwick. We have already visited the city's cathedral but this is not the only haunted historic building in Coventry. Not far from the cathedral is St Mary's Hall, a magnificent 14th-century guildhall now open to the public. St Mary's Hall has long enjoyed an eerie reputation.

Among its ghosts is a woman dressed in grey who makes her way down a staircase into the medieval kitchen. Another female phantom, this time dressed in black, has also been glimpsed in the kitchen, apparently going about the mundane task of washing dishes in the sink. The woman in black has also been seen at the foot of the stairs which lead into the Great Hall. On one occasion, an electrician working in the kitchen looked up to see himself observed by a man standing near the undercroft. Moments later the man vanished before his eyes.

The old Council Chamber is haunted by a man dressed in the scarlet robes of one of the three guilds that founded St Mary's Hall, the Trinity Guild. A figure in a long gown or dress – it could be male or female – has been glimpsed in the Minstrels' Gallery. It may be the same presence which is heard to walk along the gallery, the floorboards creaking under the weight of its feet, although no one is visible.

An inexplicable din has been known to emanate from the Old Mayoress's Parlour, as if someone inside is chucking the furniture about. Whenever anyone investigates, the sounds instantly cease, and the room is found to be in perfect order. This is the room in which Mary, Queen of Scots was temporarily imprisoned in the 16th century.

In 1985 a remarkable photograph was taken of the Great Hall from the Minstrels' Gallery which revealed, when developed, a very strange apparition standing among the scores of people attending a banquet. Professional photographer Haddon Davies took several images to record the event, including one where the attendees were standing by their tables, heads bowed while an official said grace before the meal began. When he looked at the negative, Mr Davies was astounded to see a weird figure standing in a corner close to the top table. It was gigantic, at least a head and shoulders higher than anyone else, and appeared to be wearing a hood and some sort of breastplate.

Thanks to the kindness of Janet Bord at the Fortean Picture Library, I have had the opportunity to view a large glossy print

An early 19th-century engraving of St Mary's Hall, almost certainly the most haunted place in Coventry.

developed by Mr Davies. I can confirm that the stranger is as clear as any of the banqueters and there appears to be a skull within the hood. Other people interpret the 'skull' as something resembling a gas mask. I confess to having felt a chill while I examined this puzzling photo.

St Mary's Hall is just one of the many haunted locations recorded in David McGrory's *Haunted Coventry*, an exceptionally well-researched volume containing plenty of testimony of a wide variety of ghosts around the city. Another ancient site highlighted by Mr McGrory is Whitefriars, a medieval monastery which was used as a workhouse during the 19th century. The monks belonged to the Carmelite order, who wore white – hence the name. Only the cloisters remain today. Legend has it a burly monk cracked the Devil over the head with a big stick when he was caught in these cloisters, trying to sneak in and cause trouble.

During its time as workhouse, the dormitory (now gone) was haunted by Lady Hales. The Hales family acquired Whitefriars after the Dissolution of the Monasteries and converted part of it into a private home. This particular Lady Hales was unfortunate enough to be killed, along with her maid, by a cannonball blasted into the house by Royalist forces during the Civil War. Her ghost had the habit of wandering through the dormitory at night, casting mournful looks at the residents in their beds. On at least one occasion, her appearance was intended as a warning of a coming death at the workhouse.

'I seed it, I seed it!' exclaimed one elderly witness. 'It walked three times up the room and three times down the room, and then pointed the first skinny finger of its bony right hand towards old Molly, and beckoned towards the cemetery on the road out there, so we knowed she was going to die soon.'

By contrast, Rupert Matthews highlights a much more modern location in his *Haunted Places of Warwickshire*. This is the Aston Court Hotel, now rebranded as the Days Hotel, on Holyhead Road. According to Mr Matthews, the hotel is possessed of a number of ghosts despite being only a few decades old. The most prominent of these is believed to be the spirit of a maid who, treated badly by a former manager, has taken an eternal dislike to the male sex. She makes a nuisance of herself by hiding tools and personal items belonging to male guests and staff but never targets women. Any minor misfortune suffered by a male member of staff, such as a trip or other accident, was at one time habitually blamed on this irritable spook.

Heading east from Coventry towards Northamptonshire, we come to Rugby. The Rugby Theatre in Henry Street is owned

Ghosts ancient and modern haunt the city of Coventry.
iStock

by am-dram enthusiasts who put on their own shows here. Apparently, there are two ghosts in the theatre. The backstage area is the haunt of an old actor who loved performing at the theatre so much that his spirit has chosen to revisit it from time to time. The ghost occasionally encountered roaming the auditorium is not so happy, however, for it is said to be of a member of the audience who tumbled out of the balcony and fell to his death among his fellow punters below.

In the northernmost part of Warwickshire is the county's biggest settlement, Nuneaton. The town gets its name from a medieval nunnery, of which very little now survives. The town grew in importance with the Industrial Revolution: the construction of the Coventry Canal, then the creation of an important railway junction, together with the proximity of extensive coalfields, all made Nuneaton ideal as a base for manufacturing.

Albion Buildings on the industrial estate off the Attleborough Road were used by silk and ribbon weavers in the 19th century and continue to be used for light manufacturing today. The mischievous spirit of a silk weaver is said to still haunt Albion Buildings, moving office equipment around and turning the lights off and on. In the centre of town, on Abbey Street, a pub was at one time visited by the apparition of an old lady dressed in the fashions of the Victorian period. On one occasion she was spotted by a landlord walking through a wall. Formerly the Bull's Head, the building now accommodates an Indian restaurant.

Stratford-upon-Avon is the most visited of all Warwickshire's towns and that, of course, is mainly down to one man: William Shakespeare. On Henley Street can be found the house in which the 'Bard of Avon' was born. Shakespeare's Birthplace

WARWICKSHIRE
Ghost Stories

Shakespeare's Birthplace in Stratford-upon-Avon is haunted by a sweet old lady, but whether she is a relative or descendant of the playwright is unknown. iStock

WARWICKSHIRE
Ghost Stories

is haunted by a friendly ghost. She is described by the author of *Haunted Warwickshire*, Meg Atkins, as 'a small old lady with snow-white hair and rosy cheeks, wearing an old-fashioned black dress and a black cap'. She appears in an upstairs room, sitting at a spinning wheel. On one occasion in the 1940s she suddenly materialised in front of a group of startled visitors. Smiling sweetly, she said, 'Good day, my dears,' and then vanished.

Nearby there formerly stood one of the most celebrated inns of 18th-century England, the White Lion. Before it was demolished, the inn was spread over 16-18 Henley Street. The buildings now occupying this space are said to be haunted by a serial killer of the 1700s, the so-called 'Stratford Ripper'. In 1788 the Stratford Ripper stabbed to death and mutilated the body of a prostitute at the White Lion. Before his execution he admitted to murdering five other women. His knife-wielding spectre has allegedly chased ghost-hunters away from their investigations!

Still surviving is a handsome timber-framed house, Hall's Croft, which once belonged to Shakespeare's eldest daughter, Susanna, and her husband, Dr Jonathan Hall. Dr Hall was Stratford's most esteemed physician and Hall's Croft now showcases a display of his surgical equipment, apothecary's bottles and books, including his own medical notes, published in 1657. To the rear of the building there is a Tudor garden where many of the fragrant herbs that would have been used by Dr Hall are still grown. The ghostly figure sporting an Elizabethan ruff which has been seen peering down from a first-floor window may well be the apparition of this medical gentleman.

Dr Hall – if it is he – is not the only ghost to haunt Hall's Croft. Betty Leggett shared the house with her sister in the years before the First World War but died in a fall down the stairs. Her spirit has been blamed for the uncomfortable sensation some visitors have felt when descending the stairs – a sharp push in the back by invisible hands. Is has been suggested that this is Betty's way of communicating that her 'accident' had in fact been murder.

Oddly, the staircase is also haunted by the sounds of footsteps running up and down in a lively manner. They appear to belong to the small feet of children and are unlikely to be related to the tragedy that befell Betty Leggett.

Among Stratford's many other historic buildings is the Shrieve's House in Sheep Street. This too is open to the public and contains an exhibition on life in Tudor England. Dating from the early 1500s, the property is named after its earliest known tenant, William Shrieve. Shrieve, who was an archer in the service of Henry VIII, is thought to be the identity of the apparition that is the building's most frequently seen ghost. Shrieve's House has proved a popular venue for ghost hunts in recent years and many other spooks have allegedly been identified here. The staff blame the mysterious moving around of objects overnight on the spirit of a mischievous young girl. But by far the most alarming ghost claimed for Shrieve's House is 'a dark hooded figure with red glowing eyes' which has been seen looming out of the darkness.

Finally, we must consider 'Lucy', who has the distinction of haunting a number of different locations around Stratford-upon-Avon. Lucy was supposedly an unfortunate child who, pronounced dead after a fever, was sold by her poverty-stricken parents to a doctor who wanted to dissect her body. But she

Hall's Croft, Stratford, is haunted by several spooks, including a gentleman in Elizabethan dress. iStock

wasn't dead, merely unconscious. The consequences of this error are too horrible to contemplate. The girl's remarkably cheerful spirit (considering the circumstances) turns up in various places in the town centre. One source states that in life Lucy had been a pickpocket, and witnesses have reported feeling her icy little fingers tugging at rings on their fingers and attempting to remove coins from their pockets.

Royal Leamington Spa became one of England's most fashionable resorts in the early 19th century, resulting in a legacy of elegant squares and grand Georgian buildings. Its most haunted building is its railway station, however. So many ghosts are allegedly encountered here that a 'Supernatural Liaison Officer' was appointed just before Hallowe'en in 2014. Nick Rees told the press on his appointment that staff and commuters regularly encounter apparitions both inside the building and on the platforms.
The most haunted areas are a disused basement on Platform 3 and a top-floor office where 'staff regularly see and hear things, including doors slamming, and electrical equipment turning on and off'. One worker reported: 'I regularly have paperwork thrown about, drawers left open and hear footsteps.'

In the centre of town can be found the site of the old Woodwards' department store. Only its frontage remains, the store having been demolished to make way for apartments. For many years it was claimed that the store's top floor was haunted by a woman nicknamed 'Annie' by the staff, but whose identity was never established. One morning security guards arrived to find chaos in the soft furnishings department. Cushions and other items were scattered all over the place. There was no evidence of a break-in, and nothing had been stolen. Staff wondered whether a poltergeist had been at work.

More disturbing was the occasion when a child was heard frantically screaming from inside a locked cupboard in a basement. When the cupboard was opened, the crying ceased and it was found to be empty.

Between Leamington and Redditch is the pretty little town of Henley-in-Arden. Originally a hamlet buried in the Forest of Arden, Henley began to thrive in the 13th century after Queen Matilda granted rights to a market in nearby Beaudesert Castle. A good many of its buildings survive from the medieval period. The White Swan Hotel in the High Street dates from about the year 1600, but is thought to stand on the site of an even earlier inn. For some years the hotel was claimed to be haunted by the apparition of 'a young lady of dubious virtue' (to quote Julia Skinner in her *Haunted Warwickshire: Ghost Stories*) named Virginia Black. In 1845 Virginia got into a violent row

The White Swan Hotel in Henley-in-Arden is haunted by 'a young lady of dubious virtue'. iStock

with a man and in the fracas fell – or was pushed – down the stairs. After her death, her ghost took to haunting the corridor outside the room where she used to 'entertain' her clients.

Alcester is another attractive little town, notable for its Georgian architecture. Alcester started life as a major Roman fort, later developing into an important medieval market town with its own Benedictine abbey. It even became something of an industrial centre, hard though that is to believe today, becoming famous for its ironworks in the early Middle Ages.

We have already visited Alcester's parish church as one of the places said to be haunted by Sir Fulke Greville. Opposite the church is a row of elegant Georgian houses, one of which bears on its frontage a white plaster plaque moulded into the shape of two angels. Now a private home, this is the former Angel Inn. In the 1690s a 'villain to the bone' named Captain Hill put up here. Unknown to the landlord, he was flying from justice, having murdered a young man who was favoured by an actress he fancied. His polished manner charmed everyone and his fine clothes and heavy purse were enough to make him immediately popular in Alcester. Soon after his arrival he was invited to a get-together at Churchill House, a handsome brick building which stands on the other side of the church. At the close of the evening, they played cards – and Captain Hill was found to be cheating. Furious at being found out, Hill immediately drew his sword and attacked the man who had exposed him. Fortunately, he failed to injure him, was disarmed and was thrown out of the house.

Back at the Angel Inn, the disgraced Hill continue to drink, swearing and muttering under his breath, vowing vengeance on the good people of Churchill House. But the next day he was found missing from the inn. Here begins a mystery. It was assumed Hill had simply done a bunk, escaping the town where his villainy had been exposed before word of it reached London, where he was a wanted man. It hardly needs stating that he failed to pay his bill! One account suggests that he rode west and died in 'a ghoul-haunted woodland' at Beoley, near Redditch. However, the persistent ghost stories attached to the Angel Inn suggest otherwise.

Soon after Captain Hill disappeared, rumours began to circulate that the inn had become haunted. One woman staying at the Angel with her husband reported a sleepless night in which she was troubled by strange noises, including a thump as if a body had struck the floor, and violent rocking and moving about of various items of furniture. On complaining of her experience the following morning, she learnt that a guest in the adjoining room had also had a

The former Angel Inn, in the middle of the picture, is Alcester's best-known haunted house. The plaque depicting two angels can be seen high up on the wall. iStock

disturbed night. This guest had heard the thump too and, worse still, had seen something she described as 'a tremulous mist, oval in shape' gliding past her bed. Subsequent reports refer to the 'phosphorescent image of a man' in the Angel Inn.

By about 1800, the Angel had closed its doors to the public and had become a private home. While the interior was being remodelled, a bricked-up oven was discovered. Inside were two swords and a box containing the mouldering remains of a military cloak, a felt hat, shoe buckles and a yellow vest, along with a few almost illegible, crumbling letters. The name 'Captain Richards' was decipherable on one of the letters, and this was an alias known to have been used by Captain Hill while on the run. If these were Hill's belongings, why were they hidden and what was the significance of the two swords? Surely Hill would not have gone anywhere without his sword? To the people of Alcester, here was the clue that Hill had never left the Angel, that death had come upon him here. Perhaps he was killed by one of the men he had insulted at Churchill House, or vengeance for his earlier misdeeds may have caught up with him at the inn. At any rate, no one now doubted the identity of the ghost.

In later years it was declared that a phantom wearing very much the sort of outfit outlined above had taken to haunting the vicinity of the old Angel Inn; sometimes in the house itself but also on the road outside. The ghost has been described as 'stomping down the street', while emitting a harsh, scornful laugh, unpleasant to hear.

Churchill House, the scene of Hill's gambling fracas, is also haunted but apparently by an unrelated ghost. A woman wearing the fashions of the 18th century haunts an old oak staircase between the first and second floors of the house.

Sometimes her high heels have been heard tapping on the stairs.

The last town to visit on this spooky itinerary is Southam, in the east of Warwickshire. One more example of the charming little market towns the county is blessed with, Southam has a couple of haunted properties and is the subject of an unusual story in which a ghost figured in a court case. On Market Hill there stands the old Manor House of Southam, where King Charles I lodged before the Battle of Edge Hill in 1642. This handsome gabled building has now been converted into commercial premises. Mysterious footsteps have been heard for many years striding along an upstairs corridor in the part of the building that is now used as a pharmacy, and then down a wooden staircase in the motorcycle shop next door. There is no extant story to explain them.

Another magnificent old building is the medieval Old Mint on Coventry Street. Charles I cost the people of Southam quite a lot of money: when he arrived, he fined the townsfolk for not ringing the bells to welcome his arrival, and when he came back from Edge Hill he forced them all to give up their silverware so that he could turn it into coin and pay his army. The building where the silver was melted down and coined became known ever afterwards as the Old Mint. It is now a pub. It too is said to be haunted, but by something rather vague and undefined. An old mill which stood close to the town was at one time haunted by a woman who, in time-honoured fashion, would walk around with her head tucked underneath her arm.

In 1820 a Southam farmer went missing on his return from market. A few days later his frantic wife was visited by a stranger, who broke the grave news to her that her husband was dead and that he knew this because his ghost had appeared before him. He said the farmer's spirit had told him he had been stabbed to death by a man named Peter Thomas, who then buried his body in a marl pit. The body was searched for, found, and discovered to have stab wounds corresponding to the relation of his murder by the 'ghost'. Peter Thomas was arrested and put on trial. The judge, however, pointed out that Thomas was a man of good reputation who had no reason to harm the farmer, and his only accuser was the alleged spirit of

Churchill House, Alcester, where Captain Hill caused further trouble. Like the Angel Inn, it too is said to be haunted. iStock

the deceased. He very properly ruled that the accusation of the ghost was only hearsay, unless it would appear and give its evidence before the court.

In a remarkable scene, the ghost was formally and solemnly summoned three times to appear in court. It failed to do so. The judge threw the case out of court and released Thomas. Then he directed the officers of the court to arrest the man who had caused all the trouble for him in the first place. The so-called ghost-seer was seized and later confessed to killing the farmer himself.

RURAL HAUNTINGS

Warwickshire is a largely rural county, so it's not surprising to find that a number of its ghosts are found out in the open air. One such haunted spot is Blacklow Hill, between Leek Wootton and Warwick. Here, in 1312, the favourite of King Edward II, Piers Gaveston, the 1st Earl of Cornwall, was beheaded by the Earl of Warwick. Edward was an unpopular king with his barons, often ignoring their needs and counsel, while listening instead to the waspish tongue of his favourite.

In 1312 several barons rose up against King Edward. The Earl of Cornwall was given the task of defending Scarborough Castle in Yorkshire, and did a good job, but eventually he ran out of supplies and had to yield. Gaveston had earned himself the hatred of many powerful people, not least the Earl of Warwick, whom he had nicknamed 'the Black Dog of Arden' in reference to his shaggy dark hair and beard. Gaveston was promised safe conduct back to London, but halfway down the Earl of Warwick intervened and took charge of his hated rival. Gaveston was made a prisoner in Warwick Castle and the following morning he was dragged up Blacklow Hill behind a horse. On the summit he was summarily executed, in a move that shocked even the rebellious barons.

This grim procession is said to still be played out in ghostly form, along the path to the summit of Blacklow Hill. Sometimes the jingling of bells can be heard. The horse which dragged Gaveston to his death was said to have been festooned with ribbons and little tinkling bells to further mock the unfortunate royal favourite. In 1821 a monument, called Gaveston's Cross, was erected on the spot where he lost his life. Its inscription does little to honour him, however: it bluntly describes the defunct Earl of Cornwall as 'the minion of a hateful king'.

A mysterious light has been reported from Burton Dassett Hill, near the Oxfordshire border. The spook was first written about in 1924, after a series of sightings, by the then president of the Folklore Society, A.R. Wright. He noted: 'A "ghost light", a yellow and blue ray, has been seen to flit over the lonely range of hills between [Fenny Compton] and Burton Dassett. Many people have been scared it by it.'

Meg Atkins gathered many more witness reports on the light for her book on *Haunted Warwickshire*. She learnt of three local men who saw the light on Burton Dassett Hill in 1923. They described it as being 'strong and dazzling, of a very beautiful mingled blue and red, moving at great speed between bushes and over trees and occasionally pausing to hover'. They watched as it took on an orange colour and vanished behind Burton Dassett church. The light also took to appearing in the churchyard at Burton Dassett and also in the village of Fenny Compton and over a pool beside the road leading into Northend. A group of men who

The beheading of Piers Gaveston, from an old print. The ghostly re-enactment of Gaveston's final moments is said to still be seen on Blacklow Hill. iStock

encountered the light while walking over the hills stated that they not only saw but also 'felt' it passing over them.

There is no doubt that today we would tend to consider the phenomenon as a UFO rather than a ghost. But at the time the light was said to be a lantern carried by the restless spirit of a girl called Jenny. She is supposed to appear before benighted travellers, waving her lantern in an encouraging way, leading them on through the dark. Sometimes the girl herself is seen, beckoning with her hand. However, Jenny is not a kind ghost, and she does not lead travellers on to the right path but rather away from it, taking them on a merry dance through the countryside until they are hopelessly lost. Then she vanishes. As well as UFOs, Jenny bears similarity with a kind of fairy that appears in widespread folklore with the same annoying habit of leading people astray in the dark.

Another spook related to fairy-lore is the Dun Cow. The Dun Cow was sent by the fairies to help the people of Preston-on-Stour during a famine. It was able to provide an unlimited supply of milk, but would allow just one bucketful per person. Unfortunately, a wicked, jealous old woman decided to put an end to this prosperity. She contrived a pail with a hole in the bottom, connected to a pipe which led down into her cellar. With this apparatus she was able to milk and milk and milk the fabulous animal until eventually even it ran dry. Realising it had been tricked, the Dun Cow became furious. It kicked over the bucket, gored the evil old woman to death and then attacked all the villagers. Afterwards it returned to fairyland, but its ghost, glowing with an unearthly light, was said to still manifest from time to time around Preston, a dangerous and vengeful spectre. The Dun Cow also haunts Dunsmore Heath, south-west of Rugby.

We have already visited the haunted church at Ilmington. The fields around the village are also haunted, by the eerie sound of baying hounds. Centuries ago, tradition states, a man was so fond of hunting that he would even ride to hounds on the Sabbath. As a divine punishment, one Sunday he called out his hounds as usual but they treated him as their quarry and tore him to pieces. Their ghosts and his are now doomed to hunt till Doomsday.

On one of the lanes leading out of the hamlet of Oldbury, a figure in old-fashioned clothing has been seen staggering about drunkenly. No matter how calm the night, he looks as if he is striving against a gale, his clothes whipping about him. This is the ghost of an old man who drunk a few too many in the Blue Bell pub (now a private home) while summoning up his courage to brave a storm that was howling all around. Eventually, he was turned out and, well sozzled, he struggled along as best he could until he was struck on the head by a chimney pot blown down from the roof of a cottage he was passing. The stricken fellow managed to make it a few more yards along the lane leading to his home but then collapsed and died.

There are a number of other haunted roads in Warwickshire. A phantom lorry still motors along the A428 through Brandon, near Coventry. In the 1950s, a lorry overturned in thick fog on a sharp bend, killing the driver. Since then, on occasions, motorists have been startled to encounter a vintage truck, headlights blazing, swinging round the bend at them, clearly out of control. As they slam on their own brakes, they watch as the lorry hurtles off the road and crashes into a field. When they run to help, however, they find there is no sign of the lorry or its wreckage.

WARWICKSHIRE
Ghost Stories

Burton Dassett Hill, the main haunt of Jenny and her ghostly lantern. iStock

Another apparition, with an identical story to the one supposed to haunt the parkland at Alscot (see the opening chapter), is said to be seen on the A3400 close to its junction with a minor road leading to Atherstone-on-Stour. A drunken farmer laid a bet with his friends one night on how fast he could ride home his new horse. As he turned his steed to gallop down the lane to Atherstone, his head collided with an overhanging branch and he was killed. Horse and rider now haunt this stretch of road. A strange tradition is attached to this ghost: it is said that if you see it once you will see it again twice more before you die.

Edge Hill has received a few mentions already in this book. It is a long escarpment in the very south-east of Warwickshire, overlooking a plain which is certainly the most haunted open space in the county. It was here, on 23 October 1642, that the first pitched battle of the English Civil War took place. It wasn't a planned battle, but occurred when King Charles the I was marching south to London from Shrewsbury with a hastily assembled army and met in Warwickshire a force of Parliamentarians who were heading north to capture him.

The Royalists gathered on Edge Hill and the King's nephew, Prince Rupert of the Rhine, took the initiative by leading a cavalry charge down the hill in order to surprise the Roundheads, who were mustering their forces below. The ensuing battle was brutal, bloody and undisciplined. It proved to be a victory for no one. Both sets of survivors slunk away, licking their wounds. It has been said that if the Battle of Edgehill (as it was spelled in those days) had been a decisive victory for either side, the Civil War would have ended there and then.

A couple of months after the battle, reports reached the king of strange phenomena taking place at Edge Hill. He sent a party of commissioners to investigate and they returned with the surprising information that the stories were true: some very strange things were indeed going on at the battlefield. Their report now survives in a book by a former Lord Nugent, who quotes from a 17th-century pamphlet. Nugent states that the ghostly goings-on were 'attested upon the oath of three officers, men of honour and discretion, and of three other gentlemen of credit, selected by the King as commissioners to report upon these prodigies.'

According to the commissioners, two phantom armies were meeting at the very place where the Royalist and Parliamentarian forces had clashed, but not on the field of battle itself, rather in the air above it. On the night of Christmas Eve, residents of the nearby village of Kineton had been alarmed to hear the thumping of approaching drums, mingled with 'the noise of soldiers, as it were, giving out their last groans'. Increasingly alarmed, the huddled group of witnesses were about to flee the scene when suddenly the vision of the Royalist and Parliamentarian forces appeared above their heads.

As the pamphlet puts it: 'Immediately, with ensigns displayed, drums beating, muskets going off, cannons discharged, horses neighing, the entrance to this game of death was one army, which gave the first charge, having the King's colours, and the other the Parliament's, and so pell-mell to it they went. Till two or three in the morning in equal scale continued this dreadful fight, the clattering of arms, noise of cannons, cries of soldiers …'

Eventually the Royalists appeared to be defeated and fled, while the Roundheads 'stayed a good space triumphing'. Then the extraordinary vision faded. This was only the first time it,

King Charles I, before the Battle of Edge Hill, painted by Sir Edwin Landseer.

or a similar apparition, was seen. The king's commissioners witnessed some of the spooky action for themselves and were able to testify to 'the identity of several of the illustrious dead, as seen among the unearthly combatants who had been well known to them, and who had fallen in the battle', confirming that this was no hoax or idle rumour.

The commissioners concluded that the apparition was the result of God's anger at the current discord in the kingdom, but the locals considered it was the result of so many bodies from the battle remaining unburied. They made it their mission to give all the casualties a decent burial, and the visitations from the aerial soldiers came to an end.

There have been much more recent reports of apparitions still being seen on the old battle site, however, in particular on its anniversary, 23 October. These include the ghosts of two of the Royalist officers involved in the scrap, Prince Rupert and Sir Edmund Verney. Verney died in the very thick of the battle, as he fought to reclaim the royal standard from the Roundheads. Just as he succeeded in grabbing the flag, his hand was hacked off. Today, it is said, the general's spirit regularly revisits Edge Hill in search of his lost hand. Prince Rupert survived the Battle of Edge Hill. Bewigged and finely arrayed, his ghost is seen galloping down the hill, mounted on a white charger.

Another spectral horse has been seen over the years near the Little and Great Grave Grounds, the hastily created burial places for those who fell in the battle. Two eerie figures, wearing cloaks and hoods, have also been seen nearby. One carries a lantern, while the other leads a big black dog.

'Fight for the Standard at the Battle of Edge Hill', a Victorian engraving of a particularly brutal episode during the Civil War. The two protagonists, Edward Verney and Prince Rupert, are said to still haunt the old battlefield. iStock

OUT NOW

BLACK COUNTRY & BIRMINGHAM Ghost Stories
CAMBRIDGESHIRE Ghost Stories
CHESHIRE Ghost Stories
CORNISH Ghost Stories
COTSWOLDS Ghost Stories
CUMBRIAN Ghost Stories
DERBYSHIRE Ghost Stories
DORSET Ghost Stories
ESSEX Ghost Stories
HAMPSHIRE & THE ISLE OF WIGHT Ghost Stories
KENT Ghost Stories
LANCASHIRE Ghost Stories
LEICESTERSHIRE Ghost Stories
LONDON Ghost Stories
LONDON UNDERGROUND Ghost Stories
NORFOLK Ghost Stories
NORTH WALES Ghost Stories
OXFORDSHIRE Ghost Stories
SCOTTISH Ghost Stories
SHROPSHIRE Ghost Stories
SOMERSET Ghost Stories
SOUTH WALES Ghost Stories
STAFFORDSHIRE Ghost Stories
SURREY Ghost Stories
SUSSEX Ghost Stories
WARWICKSHIRE Ghost Stories
WELSH CELEBRITY Ghost Stories
YORKSHIRE Ghost Stories

Coming In 2015

HEREFORDSHIRE Ghost Stories
WILTSHIRE Ghost Stories

In 2016 Look Out For

DEVON Ghost Stories
LINCOLNSHIRE Ghost Stories
NORTHUMBERLAND Ghost Stories
NOTTINGHAMSHIRE Ghost Stories

BRADWELL BOOKS

See website for more details: **www.bradwellbooks.co.uk**